The Story of King Arthur

TOM CRAWFORD

Illustrated by John Green

DOVER PUBLICATIONS, INC.
New York

DOVER CHILDREN'S THRIFT CLASSICS

EDITOR OF THIS VOLUME: THOMAS CROFTS

For James and Jennifer

Published in Canada by General Publishing Company, Ltd., 30 Lesmill Road, Don Mills, Toronto, Ontario.
Published in the United Kingdom by Constable and Company, Ltd., 3 The Lanchesters, 162–164 Fulham Palace Road, London W6 9ER.

Bibliographical Note

The Story of King Arthur is a new work, first published by Dover Publications, Inc., in 1994.

Library of Congress Cataloging-in-Publication Data

Crawford, Tom, 1941–
 The story of King Arthur / Tom Crawford ; illustrated by John Green.
  p. cm.—(Dover children's thrift classics)
 Summary: Recounts Arthur's chief adventures including his becoming King, his marriage to Guenevere, and his benevolent but troubled reign over England.
 ISBN 0-486-28347-X (pbk.)
 1. Arthurian romances—Adaptations. [1. Arthur, King. 2. Knights and knighthood—Folklore. 3. Folklore—England.] I. Green, John, 1948– ill. II. Title. III. Series.
PZ8.1.C863St 1994
398.2—dc20   94-3363
                  CIP
                  AC

Manufactured in the United States of America
Dover Publications, Inc., 31 East 2nd Street, Mineola, N.Y. 11501

Note

Tales of the legendary British monarch Arthur and his companions Merlin, Lancelot, Gawaine and others, come to us through poems, novels and ancient (often doubtful) historical accounts. Historians do speculate that a king of some military distinction, whose name was Arthur, was active in Wales in about the 6th century, but the threads of historical fact are impossible to separate totally from the great tapestry of legend and poetry in which most of these marvelous tales exist.

In this book, which is based upon Sir Thomas Malory's famous *Morte D'Arthur* (written in 1469), Arthur's chief adventures are recounted, including his becoming King, acquiring the magic sword Excalibur, his marriage to Guenevere and his benevolent but troubled reign over England. Recounted also are many of the exploits of Arthur's greatest knight, Sir Lancelot.

Contents

List of Illustrations

I

The Sword in the Stone

IT WAS a clear, cold December day, perhaps a thousand years ago or more, as Sir Ector and his two sons, Sir Kay and Arthur, made their way to London. The kingdom was in terrible turmoil, for King Uther Pendragon had died and a new king had not yet been chosen. Indeed, the knights and barons of the realm were fighting bitterly among themselves over who should have that honor. Finally, the Archbishop of Canterbury summoned all the knights and lords to London at Christmas in hopes that some sign would be given as to who should be king. It was for that reason that Sir Ector and his two sons were on their way to the great city.

Before long, the walls and towers of London appeared in the distance and the little party passed through one of the city's great gates. Within a short time, all the lords, including Sir Ector, gathered in one of the great churches of London to attend services and pray for guidance in choosing a new monarch. As they left the church that morning, the nobles noticed a great square stone in the churchyard. It had not been there before. And protruding from the middle of the stone was a splendid sword, its jeweled hilt gleaming in the sun. Surrounding the sword were these words written in gold: "Whoever pulls this sword from the stone is the true king of all England." The knights gasped in wonder. What could it mean?

In no time, several men had tried to pull the sword out of the stone, but no one could budge it. "He is not yet here who can move the sword," said the Archbishop, "but surely he will soon come." With that, it was decided to hold a great tournament on New Year's Day. There would be jousting and feasting, games and much merriment, and at that time, anyone who wished could try to pull the sword from the stone.

Time passed quickly and before long, the day of the tournament had arrived. As Sir Ector, Sir Kay and Arthur rode toward the tournament grounds, Sir Kay realized he had forgotten his sword. He asked Arthur to go back and get it. But when Arthur returned to their lodgings, there was no one about, and he was unable to find Kay's sword. On his way back to the tournament, Arthur remembered the sword in the stone. Determined that Sir Kay should have a sword that day, Arthur quickly rode to the churchyard. He swung down from his horse and walked over to the stone. Quickly and easily he pulled the sword from its place. Then he remounted and rode to the tournament. There he gave Sir Kay the sword.

As soon as Kay and his father saw the sword, they knew it was the one from the stone. "How did you get this sword?" Sir Ector asked Arthur. Arthur explained how he had been unable to find Sir Kay's sword and had taken the one from the stone instead. Sir Ector bowed his head. "Now I realize that you are the true king," he said to Arthur. Arthur's mouth fell open in surprise. "But father," he said, "surely there is some mistake. How can I be king?"

Then Sir Ector explained everything, how Arthur was actually of royal blood, the son of King Uther who had died several years before. The wise old magician, Merlin, in exchange for arranging the wedding of King Uther and Arthur's mother, had demanded that King Uther give him their first-born child. When Arthur was born, the King gave him to Merlin according to the agreement. In turn, Merlin had turned the baby over to Sir Ector, commanding him to raise the child as if it were his own.

Arthur, of course, was greatly saddened to learn that Sir Ector was not his real father. He rode along in silence as they went to the Archbishop to tell him what had occurred. After his initial surprise, the Archbishop decided that the sword must be put back in the stone and Arthur be allowed to show what he had done in front of all the assembled lords. Soon the nobles were once again gathered in the churchyard. The sword was replaced in the stone. One by one the lords stepped up and tried to extract the gleaming weapon from its place. One by one they failed. No one could move it even an inch. Then it was Arthur's turn. The lords whispered among themselves as the boy stepped forward. "How could a youngster like that withdraw the sword when the strongest men in the kingdom have failed?" they asked. Then everyone grew quiet as Arthur stepped up to the stone. He grasped the sword and, with one quick pull, withdrew it easily from the stone. The lords shook their heads in astonishment. Then they became angry. They said it wasn't right for the kingdom to be ruled by a boy who was not of noble blood.

He grasped the sword and, with one quick pull,
withdrew it easily from the stone.

But, as Merlin now explained to them, Arthur *was* of noble blood, and the common people who were there said it was God's will and they would accept no one but Arthur as their king. After much argument and debate, the nobles gave in, and in due time, Arthur was crowned king of all England. Even after he had become King, however, some of the lords challenged Arthur and tried to overthrow him, but the King was fast becoming a great warrior and with skill and determination he put down the revolts that threatened his realm.

II
The Round Table

ONE DAY while out hunting in the forest with Merlin, King Arthur came upon a fierce knight who insisted on jousting with every knight who came his way. Sure enough, the knight challenged King Arthur to do battle, not knowing he was the King. Arthur agreed and the two men fought a fierce battle. In the course of the fight, Arthur's sword broke in two. Seeing his opponent had no weapon, the knight prepared to strike off King Arthur's head. Before he could do so, Merlin quickly cast a spell on the knight, causing him to fall deeply asleep. Arthur scolded Merlin for killing the knight, but Merlin assured him the fallen knight was only asleep and would soon awaken. "You are wounded, though," he told Arthur. "There is a hermit's hut nearby. He will heal your wounds."

After a few days in the hermit's care, the King felt well again. It was time to leave. As the King and Merlin rode along, the King realized he had no sword. It had been broken in the fight with the knight. Merlin said, "Follow me and you shall have a sword." Before long, they came to a beautiful lake deep in the forest. In the middle of the lake, an arm, clad all in white, held a sword aloft above the water. King Arthur stared in amazement. He had never seen anything like it before.

At the water's edge stood a beautiful young woman. "Who is that?" asked Arthur. "That is the Lady of the Lake," replied Merlin. "Go and speak kindly with her. Perhaps she will give you the sword." Arthur did as Merlin suggested and told the Lady of the Lake that his sword had been destroyed in battle and he was greatly in need of a new one. "The sword in the lake is mine but you may have it if you promise to give me a gift when I ask for it," said the Lady. "It is a strange request," said King Arthur, "but I will do as you wish." "Then take the boat you see yonder and row out to the sword. It is yours," said the Lady of the Lake. King Arthur quickly made his way across the water to the sword. It was soon in his hands—Excalibur, the finest sword he had ever seen. Its blade shone brighter than a hundred suns and it seemed to Arthur that this sword had been made just for him. As they rode off, Merlin told him to be sure and always keep the scabbard of the sword with him, for as long as he possessed it, he would never shed his blood in battle.

Several years passed. King Arthur was now a strong and handsome young man. His kingdom was at peace. He began to think about getting married, especially since the knights of the realm had been urging him to find himself a wife. "Every kingdom should have a queen," they said. King Arthur decided to talk to Merlin about it. "My barons want me to get married," Arthur told Merlin, "but I wanted to ask your advice first." "I agree with the knights," said Merlin, "a man of your rank and power should have a wife. Now is there any woman you especially love?"

"Yes," said King Arthur, "I love Guenevere, the daughter of King Leodegrance of Cameliard. He is the king who possesses the Round Table you told me he got from my father, King Uther."

"She is certainly one of the most beautiful women in the world," said Merlin, "and I can see you will have no other but her."

"It is true," replied King Arthur.

"Then I will go and see King Leodegrance and tell him of your wishes," said Merlin.

When Merlin told King Leodegrance that

King Arthur wanted to wed his daughter, King Leodegrance was overjoyed. "That is wonderful news—that a king so renowned for strength and nobility wishes to marry Guenevere. As a wedding present, I would give him land, but he already has enough land. Instead, I will give him something he will like even more—the Round Table that King Uther Pendragon gave me. Not only that," continued the King, "I will give him a hundred knights to go with it. The table is big enough to seat a hundred and fifty, but I have lost many knights in battle lately."

And so it happened that Guenevere, Merlin and the hundred knights set out for London, transporting the Round Table with them. When at last they arrived at King Arthur's court, the King was overjoyed. "I have loved this beautiful lady for a long time," he said, smiling at Guenevere, "and I am very glad she is to become my wife. What's more, I would rather have this Round Table and these noble knights as a wedding present than anything else I can think of."

With that, the King gave orders to plan the royal wedding and coronation. Then he said to Merlin, "Go and find me fifty of the finest, most noble knights in the kingdom to fill the rest of the seats at the Round Table." Within a short time, Merlin had returned with twenty-eight knights but could find no more. Then the Archbishop of Canterbury was sent for and he blessed each seat at the Round Table. After the blessing, Merlin told the assembled knights that they must arise and do homage to King Arthur, that is, they must pay the King their respects and assure him of their loyalty and devotion. After paying homage, the knights departed. And at each seat, the name of the knight was written in gold.

Shortly after, the King married Guenevere in a solemn ceremony at Saint Stephen's Church in Camelot. The wedding was followed by much feasting and merriment. Then the King called all his knights together. It was time to take their vows of allegiance to the Round Table. Glancing around the table at the assembled knights, the King told them quietly but firmly what he expected of them: that they were never to be guilty of murder or treason; that they must always grant mercy to those who asked for it; that they must always help ladies in need; and that they must stay out of quarrels and fights over goods and property. When the King had finished, a hush fell over the table. Then all the knights arose: "We swear," said the knights solemnly, "to abide by and uphold the rules and ideals of the Round Table."

It was not long after this that Merlin fell in

love with Nimue, one of the beautiful young Ladies of the Lake. He followed her around like a puppy dog and seldom let her out of his sight. For her part, Nimue put up with him while she learned many secrets from the old magician. One day, Merlin told King Arthur that, in spite of all his magic powers, he, Merlin, would not live much longer. He then predicted many things that would happen in the future. He especially warned King Arthur to keep his sword, Excalibur, and its scabbard always with him, for if he did not, Excalibur would be stolen by a woman he trusted completely.

"But, Merlin," said King Arthur, who was greatly saddened by the prospect of the old man's death, "if you know in advance how you will die, why don't you use your magic powers to escape?"

"No," said Merlin, "it cannot be." And with that he departed.

After leaving King Arthur, Merlin rejoined Nimue and the two of them traveled over the sea to the land of Benwick. At the time, the King of Benwick was fighting a fierce war against King Claudas. At the court, Merlin spoke to the King's wife, a good woman named Elaine, and saw her young son, a boy named Lancelot. Elaine told Merlin how much she was worried about the war King Claudas was waging against her husband and the kingdom.

"Don't be afraid," Merlin told her, pointing to Lancelot, "for the time will come when this boy will defeat King Claudas, and the whole world will know him as the greatest knight of all."

"O Merlin," said the Queen, "shall I live to see my son become such a great knight?"

"Indeed you will, my lady, and for many years afterward," replied Merlin.

A short time later, Merlin and Nimue left the castle and resumed their journey, arriving after a while in Cornwall. By now, Nimue was heartily sick of the old man and wanted to be rid of him, but she was afraid of his magical powers. Then one day Merlin showed her a great rock, under which he said there was a marvelous sight, placed there by magic. "You go under and tell me what is there," said Nimue. Merlin agreed and managed to wriggle under the rock. As soon as he was out of sight, Nimue cast an enchanted spell over the rock and, in spite of all his magic, Merlin was unable to escape. That was the end of the old sorcerer, just as he had foretold.

III
Morgan le Fay

BACK AT court, King Arthur was preparing for a hunting expedition with King Uriens and Sir Accolon of Gaul. When all was ready, the three men rode deep into the forest. Spotting a great red stag ahead of them in the woods, they quickly gave chase. Mile after mile they pursued the magnificent deer until their horses could go no further. The poor animals were nearly dead with exhaustion. "What will we do now?" asked King Arthur. "Let's continue on foot," replied King Uriens, "until we find someplace to refresh ourselves." So they walked on through the forest for many hours, until, finally, they came to a strange body of water. There, to their astonishment, they saw a little ship, all draped in silk, floating near the shore. King Arthur beckoned his companions. "Come, let us see what's inside," he said.

So all three boarded the mysterious vessel to have a look around. By this time it was get-

ting dark. They had no sooner entered the little ship, than a hundred torches suddenly
blazed up, lighting the walls, which were also
richly hung with silk. King Arthur, Sir Accolon
and King Uriens stood there speechless with
wonder as twelve beautiful young maidens
appeared as if from nowhere and made them
welcome.

Then the maidens led them into a dining
room where they were served the most delicious meats and wines. They ate until they
couldn't eat another mouthful. King Arthur
could not remember when he had enjoyed
such a wonderful meal. When dinner was
over, the maidens took each man to his own
bedroom. The rooms were furnished with the
most beautiful furniture and luxurious rugs
and draperies. In no time, the three exhausted
men fell fast asleep.

The next morning, to his great surprise,
King Uriens found himself back in Camelot,
with his wife, King Arthur's sister, Morgan le
Fay. He had no idea how he had gotten there.
King Arthur, on the other hand, awoke to find
himself in a dark prison. All around him,
knights were moaning and complaining. "Why
are you so unhappy?" asked King Arthur. The
knights explained that they had been imprisoned by an evil knight, Sir Damas, the owner

of the castle. This Sir Damas had a younger brother, Sir Ontzlake, who was rightfully enti- tled to a share of the castle and its lands, but Sir Damas would not share. Sir Ontzlake had offered to fight his brother for his rightful share, but Sir Damas was a coward and afraid he would lose the battle. Instead he tried to get other knights to fight for him. But know- ing Sir Damas to be evil and false, no knight would agree to it.

When Sir Damas realized none of his own knights would fight for him, he decided to capture knights traveling near the castle and imprison them until he found one who would. But even though Sir Damas promised to free the other knights if one would agree to fight Sir Ontzlake, the knights still refused. They preferred to die in prison than to do battle for such a false and treacherous man as Sir Damas.

As King Arthur pondered this unhappy situ- ation, a young woman suddenly appeared out of nowhere. "Sir," she said, "if you will fight for Sir Damas, you will be set free; if not, you will never escape!"

"That is a hard choice," replied King Arthur, "but I will fight on one condition: that if I do, all these prisoners will be set free."

"It shall be as you wish," said the young lady, preparing to leave. "But wait," cried King

Arthur, jumping to his feet, "I have no horse and no armor!"

"You shall have whatever you need," she replied, mysteriously.

The more he looked at the young woman, the more King Arthur thought he had seen her somewhere before. "Have you ever been at the court of King Arthur?" he asked. "No, I was never there," she responded. "I am the daughter of the lord of this castle." But that was not so, for in truth, she was one of the ladies who waited on Morgan le Fay.

After leaving the prison, she went straight to Sir Damas and told him that Arthur had agreed to fight for him. "Wonderful," replied Sir Damas, "have him brought here immediately." When Arthur came, he and Sir Damas agreed that Arthur should do battle for him and that the other knights were to be released. "Set the knights free," said Sir Damas to a servant, "so they can watch this noble knight take up arms against Sir Ontzlake."

In the meantime, Sir Accolon of Gaul had awakened from his sleep aboard the ship to find himself in a strange place, dangerously close to the edge of a well. "God help me!" he exclaimed, "those women on the ship were not women, they were devils!"

As Accolon thought angrily about how he,

King Arthur and King Uriens had been tricked,
a dwarf suddenly appeared at his side. The
dwarf brought greetings from Morgan le Fay
and told Sir Accolon that she wished him to
fight a certain knight early next morning. And
to help him in the fight, she had sent King
Arthur's sword, Excalibur, and its scabbard.
"Return to Morgan le Fay and tell her I will do
as she asks or die trying," Accolon told the
dwarf. "I assume she will use her sorcery to
help me win this battle." "You may count on
it," said the dwarf, and vanished as suddenly
as he had come. A few moments later, a
knight and a lady, with six squires, appeared
and whisked Accolon off to a manor to rest
and enjoy himself.

Back at his castle, Sir Damas was in a fine
mood. He sent for his brother, Sir Ontzlake,
and told him that he had found a knight to
fight with him the next morning. Unfortunately, Sir Ontzlake was in no condition to
fight; his legs had been wounded in a jousting
competition and he could not possibly do battle. Deeply disappointed, he returned to his
room. To his great surprise, he found Sir
Accolon there. Morgan le Fay had been work-
ing her magic again. Accolon told him that he
knew Sir Ontzlake was wounded and offered
to fight in his place. Sir Ontzlake could not

believe his good fortune. He accepted Accolon's offer immediately and told him that if the opportunity ever arose, he would do the same for him. With that, Sir Ontzlake sent word to Sir Damas that he had a knight who would fight for him the following day.

Bright and early the next morning, King Arthur put on his armor and mounted his horse. As he prepared to make his way to the jousting field, a young woman suddenly appeared in the courtyard. "I come from Morgan le Fay," said the woman; "she asked me to bring you your sword, Excalibur." Arthur was a little surprised at this, but he took the sword, thanked her for her trouble and rode off. Little did he know that the treacherous Morgan le Fay had deceived him a second time.

When King Arthur arrived at the battlefield, the other knight was already there. When all was ready, each man rode to the opposite end of the field. A shrill trumpet blast sounded and the two knights charged toward each other, their spears lowered. Crash! King Arthur and Accolon hit each other in the shields with their spears so hard that both men were knocked from their horses. Still dizzy from the force of the blows, they slowly staggered to their feet and drew their swords.

King Arthur and Accolon hit each other so
hard that both men fell from their horses.

Again they charged toward each other, thrusting and slashing with all their might. As they fought, a beautiful woman appeared along the sidelines. It was Nimue, the Lady of the Lake, who had put Merlin under the stone. She knew that Morgan le Fay had arranged it so that Arthur would be killed that day and she had come to save him if she could.

Meanwhile, Arthur and Accolon were fighting like furies, dealing each other mighty blows, each trying to gain the upper hand. But something was terribly wrong! It seemed to Arthur that his sword was dull and heavy. Even when he hit Accolon as hard as he could, it had little effect. Accolon's sword, on the other hand, was having a great deal of effect. Dancing in Accolon's hand, its gleaming razor-sharp blade blinded Arthur with its bright light and before he knew it, Arthur had been wounded many times.

A feeling of dread came over the King. The ground was sprinkled everywhere with his blood. If the fight continued this way, he was sure to die. Still, he fought back as hard as he could. He was a brave and strong man and he would not give up. Gathering all the strength he had left, he struck Accolon a mighty blow on the helmet. Accolon staggered backward, struggling to keep his feet. But his heart leapt with joy at what he saw then: Arthur's sword had split in two from the force of the blow. The blade dropped useless into the grass.

"Knight," cried Accolon, "you are at my mercy. You have no weapon and you have lost much blood. You must surrender to me or die!"

"Never," replied King Arthur coldly and calmly. "I have sworn on my honor to fight to the death. And even though I have no weapon, I would rather die a hundred deaths with honor than surrender in shame."

"Very well," said Accolon, advancing with his sword upraised, "if that is what you wish, then prepare to die right now!" But the Lady of the Lake could not bear to see Arthur killed, for she loved the noble king. So, just as Accolon was about to strike off King Arthur's head, she cast a spell on him, causing him to drop his sword. Quick as a cat, Arthur leaped on it. "Knight," he cried, "you have cost me much pain and blood with this sword. Now you must die by it." With that he rushed upon Accolon and felled him with one mighty blow. Pulling off Accolon's helmet, Arthur made ready to cut off his head. "Kill me if you wish," said the fallen knight, "for you are the finest warrior I have ever fought. But I, too, promised to battle to the death. I can never surrender!"

As he gazed at the man, Arthur thought he recognized his face. "Who are you and where are you from?" he asked. "I am of King Arthur's court and my name is Accolon of Gaul," the knight replied. Arthur shook his head in amazement, beginning to connect his sister Morgan le Fay with the enchanted ship. "O knight," he said, "I beg of you to tell me where you got this sword and from whom."

"I am deeply ashamed that I used this sword, for I think it will mean my death," said Accolon softly. "It was sent to me by Morgan le Fay, King Uriens' wife. She wanted me to kill her brother, King Arthur."

"But why should she want to kill him?" asked King Arthur, shocked by these words. "She hates her brother more than any man in the world," replied Accolon, "because she is jealous of his great power and influence."

"Continue," said King Arthur, eager to know more about this strange plot. "Morgan le Fay loves me and I love her," declared Accolon defiantly. "Through her magic powers she has arranged for me to kill King Arthur. When Arthur is dead, she will kill her husband, King Uriens, and make me king in his place. Then Morgan le Fay will be queen.

"But now all is lost," cried Accolon, burying his face in his hands. After a moment, Accolon raised his head. "I have told you everything," he said to King Arthur, still unaware of his foe's identity, "now I would like to know who *you* are."

King Arthur raised the visor on his helmet. He spoke sternly: "Accolon, I am Arthur, your King, and you have severely wounded me."

Accolon gasped in astonishment. "My lord, I beg you for mercy. I did not know it was you!" Then he hung his head in shame.

"You shall have mercy," replied King Arthur, "for I honestly believe you did not know who you were fighting just now. But you *did* plan to kill me, which makes you a traitor. You deserve to be put to death, but I forgive you because I know you fell under the evil spell of my sister, Morgan le Fay."

With that, King Arthur swore to avenge himself on his traitorous sister, whom he had always honored and trusted above anyone else.

Then, turning to Sir Damas, King Arthur told him he was an evil, brutal man who had tortured and imprisoned innocent knights. As a punishment, King Arthur awarded the castle and the entire estate to Sir Ontzlake. After commanding that all prisoners be freed, King Arthur invited Sir Ontzlake to come to Camelot and be one of the Knights of the Round Table.

"God bless you," replied Sir Ontzlake. "I shall always be at your service."

At last, it was time to go. Unfortunately, King Arthur and Accolon were still suffering from their wounds. They needed a place to rest before they returned to Camelot.

Sir Ontzlake directed them to a nearby abbey where the nuns would let them stay while their wounds healed. But Accolon had lost too much blood. After four days at the abbey, he died. King Arthur was luckier. He recovered from his wounds and became stronger every day. After Accolon's death, he directed that the body be sent back to Camelot.

"Take him to my sister, Morgan le Fay," said King Arthur. "Tell her that I send her a present, and that I have recovered my sword Excalibur and the scabbard."

When Morgan le Fay discovered that Accolon was dead, she was broken-hearted, but she kept her grief to herself so that no one else knew how much it hurt. At the same time, she knew she had to leave Camelot. If she was still there when King Arthur returned, her life would be in great danger.

Early the next morning, Morgan le Fay mounted her horse and rode all day until she reached the abbey where King Arthur was staying. Morgan le Fay asked the nuns in charge where he was. They told her he was sleeping and should not be awakened. Morgan le Fay promised not to disturb him and silently stole into his bedchamber. She hoped to steal the sword Excalibur while the King slept. To her dismay, Morgan le Fay saw that King Arthur's hand grasped his sword, even in his sleep. She knew she could not get Excalibur without waking him. Then she spied the scabbard standing in the corner. Quickly and silently, she snatched it up and slipped from the room.

When King Arthur awoke, he immediately realized the scabbard was gone. "Who has been in my room?" cried the furious King. The nuns told him his sister, Morgan le Fay, had been there but she was gone. "Ah, she has tricked me again," moaned Arthur. "We must catch her!" With that, the King summoned Sir Ontzlake, who had remained at the abbey with him. The two men hastily donned their armor, mounted their horses, and galloped furiously away in pursuit of Arthur's treacherous sister.

It was not long before they caught sight of Morgan le Fay and a group of knights far in the distance across a wide plain. "There she is!" cried Arthur, "after her!" But as they thundered across the plain, the sound of their horses' hooves caused Morgan le Fay to look back. She knew instantly who it was. "It is my brother!" exclaimed the Queen. "If he catches me, he will kill me! We must hurry!"

Morgan le Fay and her followers spurred their horses and galloped off in a great cloud of dust. After passing through a forest, they came to a small, gloomy lake. Morgan le Fay stopped her horse and jumped down. "Whatever happens to me, King Arthur shall not have this scabbard!" she cried, and hurled it into the deep, murky water. Heavy with gold and precious jewels, the scabbard immediately sank out of sight. The Queen then remounted and rode on.

But soon she again heard the hoofbeats of pursuing horses. This time they seemed closer than ever. She must do something quickly! Morgan le Fay, of course, was a sorceress who possessed many magic powers. She called on those powers now to save her life. In a twinkling, she changed herself, her horse and her followers into a cluster of large rocks, just like the others in the valley around them. When King Arthur and Sir Ontzlake arrived, still in hot pursuit, Morgan le Fay was nowhere to be found. "Tricked again," grumbled King Arthur, knowing his sister had once more outwitted him. "We won't find her now. Let's return to the abbey."

As soon as they had gone, Morgan le Fay reversed the magic spell. When everything was back to normal, she said, with a contented little smile on her lips, "Now we may travel wherever we wish. Let us go to the land of Gore." When they arrived in that country, Morgan le Fay was greeted with cheers and shouts by the people, who did not know of her evil ways. While she was there, she took special care to strengthen her castles for she feared that sooner or later King Arthur would attack.

Meanwhile, King Arthur had left the abbey and returned to Camelot. Queen Guenevere and the Knights of the Round Table welcomed him back with great joy. When they heard about the evil deeds of Morgan le Fay, they marveled at her treachery and many wished her burned at the stake. But, of course, Morgan le Fay had escaped and no one knew where she was.

Not long after, a young woman arrived at Camelot. She brought with her the most beautiful cloak ever seen in that kingdom. It was made of rich, luxurious fabrics and studded with diamonds, rubies and emeralds. The young woman presented the cloak to King Arthur. "Your sister sends this cloak as a gift.

She is deeply sorry for any trouble she has caused and she wants you to have the cloak with her apologies," said the maiden, a mysterious smile playing about her mouth. King Arthur was speechless with astonishment. It was the most magnificent garment he had ever seen. He longed to try it on.

But just as he reached for the cloak, a golden mist swirled before his eyes and the Lady of the Lake appeared out of nowhere. "Sir," she whispered, "whatever you do, do not wear that cloak until the maiden that brought it puts it on first. I beg of you!" The King stared at her in amazement. What possible harm could there be in trying on a cloak? Nevertheless, she had saved his life before and it might be a good idea to do as she said.

Turning to the maiden, King Arthur told her to put on the cloak. A look of dread stole across her face. "Oh no, Sir," she cried, "I could not possibly wear a cloak meant for a king!" But King Arthur would not be denied. "You must wear it first or no one will wear it!" thundered the King. Finally, after many protests, the trembling girl pulled on the cloak. No sooner had she wrapped it about herself than she fell dead to the floor. In an instant, nothing remained of her body but a small heap of glowing coals.

With a cry of rage and pain, King Arthur

turned to King Uriens. "Your wife, my sister, is always trying to have me killed. I would suspect you of being involved, too, except that I know she planned to kill you as well!" With that, the angry King stormed out of the hall.

IV

Sir Lancelot's First Adventures

SOME TIME after his close call with the deadly cloak, King Arthur held a great tournament at Camelot. Knights from all over the realm came to take part in the jousting and feasting. It was a warm spring day and the air rang with the sound of clashing spears and swords as armored knights rode against each other in furious combat. As the day wore on, one knight stood out above all others. He not only defeated every knight he fought, he was modest in victory and kindly toward his fallen foes. Before long, his name was on everyone's lips.

The name of the noble knight was Lancelot, the very same young boy Merlin had seen so many years before in the land of Benwick. Now grown tall and strong, he had been at court several years. Everyone agreed he was the greatest Knight of the Round Table. He was especially favored by Queen Guenevere. She loved him more than any other knight and Sir Lancelot loved and respected her in turn.

After the tournament was over, Sir Lancelot rested and enjoyed himself at court for a time. But soon he grew restless. Perhaps it would be a good idea to go in search of adventures beyond the walls of Camelot. He invited his nephew, Sir Lionel, to join him. Soon the two knights had ridden their horses through the city gates and left the towers and spires of Camelot far behind.

It was a beautiful sunny morning. Birds sang in the trees all about them and the road wound away toward the misty blue hills in the distance. After riding for several hours, they stopped to rest. The heat had made Sir Lancelot very sleepy. He lay down under an apple tree with his helmet for a pillow and was soon fast asleep. Sir Lionel kept watch. Before long, three mounted knights came into view, hotly pursued by one of the biggest, strongest knights Sir Lionel had ever seen. As he watched in amazement, the great knight caught up with the other three knights and knocked them off their horses one by one. Then he tied them up with their own bridles.

After seeing those knights so badly beaten, Sir Lionel could not sit still. He decided to challenge the great knight himself. Quietly, so as not to wake Sir Lancelot, he picked up his spear and mounted his horse. Once out of earshot, Sir Lionel challenged the other knight in a loud voice. Instantly, his powerful foe wheeled around and charged forward. Almost before he knew what had happened, Sir Lionel found himself lying dazed on the ground, knocked from his saddle with one mighty blow of the knight's spear. Before he could move, the knight leaped on him and quickly tied Sir Lionel up just like the others. Then the great knight threw his four captives over their saddles and led them all off to his castle. There, they were soundly beaten and thrown into prison. All around him in the dark and dirty dungeon, Sir Lionel heard other knights moaning in pain and despair.

In the meantime, Sir Lancelot was still sound asleep under the apple tree, unaware that Sir Lionel had been captured and taken away. As he slept, four great queens approached, riding on white mules. Four knights rode with them, holding a green silk cloth aloft with their spears to shade the queens from the hot sun. When they got a little closer, the queens recognized Sir Lancelot stretched out under the tree. Immediately they began squabbling over who should have him. "Let us not argue now," said one of the queens, who happened to be Morgan le Fay, King Arthur's evil sister. "I will put a spell on

The queens recognized Sir Lancelot stretched out
under the tree.

him and take him back to my castle. Once he is my prisoner, I will remove the spell and he can then choose which of us he wants."

The other queens agreed, and in no time Morgan le Fay had cast a spell over the sleeping knight. Two of her knights laid Sir Lancelot on his shield and carried him back to her castle. There he was locked alone in a damp and cold stone chamber. Sir Lancelot could hear rats scurrying in the dark corners. That evening, a young maiden brought his supper. By this time, the enchantment had worn off and Sir Lancelot was very curious about where he was and how he had gotten there. "I can't tell you anything now," whispered the girl, "but I will explain everything tomorrow." Then she left, leaving Sir Lancelot to puzzle over his fate.

Early the next morning, the four queens came to his room. "Sir knight," one began, "we know you are Lancelot, the greatest knight in the realm, and that you love only Queen Guenevere. But you are our prisoner and you cannot have her. Therefore, you must choose one of us." His eyes wide with disbelief, Lancelot was too shocked to reply. The Queen continued: "I am Morgan le Fay, Queen of the land of Gore; over there are the Queen of Northgalis, the Queen of Eastland and the

Queen of the Out Isles. Now you must choose one of us or die in this prison."

"This is a hard choice," replied Sir Lancelot, "but I would rather die in prison than to choose a woman I do not love."

"Then you are refusing us?" asked Morgan le Fay, unable to believe her ears.

"Yes," replied Sir Lancelot quietly but firmly. And with that, the four angry and disappointed queens swept out of the room, leaving Sir Lancelot thinking sadly about spending the rest of his life in that lonely cell.

At noon, the same young woman came to deliver his meal. When she asked how he was, Sir Lancelot admitted he had never felt so bad. The young woman smiled. "Sir, if you will promise me one thing, I will help you escape." "Gladly," replied Lancelot, "for I am afraid of these witch-queens. They have destroyed many a good knight."

"If you promise to help my father, King Bagdemagus, at a tournament next Tuesday, I will get you out of here," said the girl.

"I know your father well as a noble king and a good knight," replied Sir Lancelot. "I would be proud to help him."

The young woman then told Lancelot to be ready early next morning, when she would come with his armor, a spear and a horse. He was then to ride to an abbey ten miles away and wait until she and her father arrived.

True to her promise, the young girl appeared the following morning and unlocked the door. Lancelot was free! Outside, his horse and armor were all ready, just as promised. As quietly as possible, he donned his armor and rode swiftly away from the castle.

He rode all day until he reached the abbey. He had no sooner arrived than the girl and her father, King Bagdemagus, rode up to the entrance. Sir Lancelot and the king exchanged warm greetings. Then King Bagdemagus explained how his knights had been badly beaten at the last tournament by three Knights of the Round Table.

"Who were they?" asked Lancelot.

"Sir Mador de la Porte, Sir Mordred and Sir Galahantine," replied the King. "Against them my knights and I could do nothing. It was humiliating. Will you help us at the next tournament?"

Remembering his promise, Sir Lancelot then agreed to fight for the King—but in disguise. "Send me three knights that you trust," said Lancelot, "and give us all white shields with no identifying marks on them. When the tournament is well underway, we will appear and fight on your side." The King was well pleased with this arrangement, and after a hearty meal, they all retired to bed.

On the day of the tournament, the battle was not going well for King Bagdemagus. A number of his knights had already been knocked from their horses and badly injured. Watching from a hiding place, Sir Lancelot decided it was time to enter the battle. Riding into the midst of the fighting, he struck down the King of Northgalis, who broke his thigh in the fall. Then Sir Mador de la Porte challenged Lancelot. The two knights rode together, their strong spears fixed in place. Crash! Sir Mador fell to the earth and lay still. Now it was Sir Mordred's turn. He armed himself with a great spear and rode directly at Sir Lancelot. When they came together, Sir Mordred's spear splintered to pieces against Lancelot's shield. Then Lancelot gave him such a blow that he flew backwards off his horse and fell to the ground unconscious.

Having watched his two companions go down to defeat, Sir Galahantine took the field. Once again Sir Lancelot prepared for battle. Their spears in place, the two knights galloped directly toward one another. This time, both their spears shattered from the force of the blows. Drawing their swords, they swung at each other with many slashing strokes. Finally, Sir Lancelot landed a great blow on

Sir Galahantine's helmet. Dazed and bloody in his saddle, Sir Galahantine lost control of his horse. The frightened animal reared up and threw Sir Galahantine from his back. He hit the ground with a great thud and did not move.

Now the tide began to turn in favor of King Bagdemagus. Sir Lancelot went on to defeat many more knights that day, and by the end of the tournament, the forces of the King of Northgalis had been thoroughly defeated. Thanks to Sir Lancelot, King Bagdemagus and his knights were declared winners of the tournament.

Back at the castle, Sir Lancelot was showered with gifts and heartfelt thanks from the king and his daughter. But in all that time, he had not forgotten Sir Lionel, who had been kidnapped while Lancelot slept. Now it was time to try and find him. Bidding his hosts a last farewell, Lancelot rode away from the castle.

It was not long before he found himself in the same forest in which Sir Lionel had disappeared. Suddenly a beautiful young maiden on a snowy white horse came into view. After greeting her, Sir Lancelot asked if she knew of any adventures in that part of the country. The maiden said she did, and that if he would tell her his name, she would take him to meet one of the strongest, most skilled knights in the realm. Lancelot told her his name.

"Sir," she replied, "you have come to the right place to find adventure, for this man is one of the strongest knights in the world. His name is Sir Turquine and he holds in his prison sixty-four knights from Arthur's court. He defeated them all himself.

"I only ask one thing," she continued. "When you are finished here, I beg you to come and help me and other maidens who are attacked every day by a treacherous knight."

Sir Lancelot agreed to do as she asked if she would first take him to Sir Turquine. "All right," she replied. Leading the way, she soon brought Lancelot to a shallow stream. Nearby, a basin hung from a tree. Sir Lancelot banged on the basin with the end of his spear to summon Sir Turquine, but there was no response. They continued on, passing by the wall of a great manor. Then, in the distance, Sir Lancelot saw a knight coming toward him. The knight was leading a horse and across the saddle an armed knight lay bound hand and foot. When they had come closer, Sir Lancelot recognized the bound knight. It was Sir Gaheris, brother of Sir Gawaine, and a Knight of the Round Table.

Sir Lancelot then addressed Sir Turquine, for it was indeed he who led the captive knight. "Take that wounded knight off the horse and let him rest. I am told you have done great harm to the Knights of the Round Table. Prepare to defend yourself!"

"If you are a Knight of the Round Table, I defy you and all your kind," sneered Sir Turquine.

"Then, you had better be ready to fight," answered Lancelot, barely controlling his anger.

The two knights then put their spears in place and galloped toward each other as fast as they could. They struck each other so hard in the midst of their shields that both horses were knocked off their feet. As the horses fell, the two knights leaped down and drew their swords.

For almost an hour, the sounds of sword on sword echoed through the forest as Sir Lancelot and Sir Turquine fought ferociously. Finally, they stopped to rest, panting and heaving. Neither had been able to get the upper hand. When he had finally caught his breath, Sir Turquine spoke with admiration: "You are the strongest knight I have ever fought, and you remind me of the one knight I hate above all others. As long as you are not he, I will agree to stop the fight now and release all the prisoners I hold."

"That is a generous offer," responded Sir

Lancelot. "But tell me, which knight is it that you hate above all others?"

"Sir Lancelot," replied Turquine, "for he killed my brother, Sir Carados, one of the best knights who ever lived. I have sworn to avenge my brother's death, and if I ever come across Sir Lancelot, I will fight him to the death. If you are not he, then we can be friends and I will let all the captive knights go free."

"Then you must know," responded Sir Lancelot, "that I am indeed the knight you seek. I am Sir Lancelot of the Round Table."

Roaring in rage, Sir Turquine raised his sword and fell upon Lancelot, determined to put an end to his sworn foe. They fought like two wild bulls, dealing each other many fearful blows, until blood sprinkled the forest floor. At last, Sir Turquine stumbled backwards a bit, lowering his shield from fatigue. Seizing his opportunity, Sir Lancelot leaped on the exhausted knight and hurled him to the ground. Ripping off Turquine's helmet, Lancelot severed his head with one mighty blow of his sword.

After Lancelot had rested a while and recovered himself from this exhausting battle, he told the young maiden he was ready to accompany her, but his horse had been injured in the fight. She suggested he take Sir Gaheris' horse. That knight was only too happy to lend Lancelot his horse, for Lancelot had saved his life. Sir Lancelot then told Sir Gaheris to go to the manor and free the knights imprisoned there, among whom were many Knights of the Round Table. "Greet them for me," Lancelot commanded Sir Gaheris, "and tell them I hope to be back at the Round Table soon, after I have helped this maiden." Waving farewell to Sir Gaheris, Lancelot and the girl on the white horse set off on a new adventure.

At the manor, Gaheris soon released all the knights and told them of everything Sir Lancelot had done. They all cheered Lancelot in his absence. Delighted to be free after many days and hours in the dark prison of Sir Turquine, the men joyfully gathered up their belongings and prepared to return to Camelot. Of all the knights, three chose not to return right away. Sir Lionel, Sir Ector and Sir Kay decided to try and find Sir Lancelot if they could.

As they rode side by side through the green forest, the maiden told Sir Lancelot about the knight who haunted these woods and robbed women passing by. "What!" cried Lancelot in disbelief, "he claims to be a knight and yet he attacks and robs women traveling on this road! He has dishonored the oath of knighthood. He must be punished."

Then Sir Lancelot had an idea. "Ride on ahead," he told the maiden, "if he troubles you, I will come to your rescue and teach him a lesson." The young woman did as she was told, and sure enough, a short way down the road, the evil knight came riding out of the bushes. Grabbing her by the cloak, he pulled the maiden off her horse. Terrified, she cried out. Sir Lancelot, who had been staying out of sight, now came at a gallop.

"O false knight," cried Sir Lancelot, "who taught you to attack women? You are a disgrace to knighthood!"

The other knight did not respond but drew his sword instead. But he was no match for the greatest knight of the Round Table. With one shattering blow, Sir Lancelot drove his sword through the knight's helmet and deep into his brain. No more would that evil knight attack and rob innocent women on the highway.

V

The Chapel Perilous and Other Adventures of Sir Lancelot

AFTER RECEIVING the grateful thanks of the maiden and saying goodbye, Sir Lancelot rode on in search of new adventures. He passed through many strange and wild places, until at last, as night was coming on, he found a cottage where he could stay for the night. The old woman who lived there served him a delicious meal and later showed him to his room on the second floor, overlooking the gate. Weary from his long ride, Sir Lancelot fell into a deep sleep. In the middle of the night he was awakened by a great commotion in the courtyard below.

Looking out the window, he saw one knight fighting for his life against three others who were attacking him with swords. "I must help that knight," said Sir Lancelot to himself, "three against one is not a fair fight." Quickly fashioning a rope from the bedsheets, Lancelot lowered himself to the ground. To his great surprise he recognized the lone knight as Sir Kay of the Round Table.

"Leave that knight alone, you villains!" he shouted, "I dare you to fight with me!" As soon as he had uttered those words, the three knights immediately dismounted their horses and attacked Sir Lancelot. But his great strength and skill with the sword proved too much for them. One after the other he struck them down. When all three had surrendered, Sir Lancelot commanded them to report to Queen Guenevere at Camelot and to throw themselves on her mercy. Having sworn on their swords that they would, the three knights quickly left the scene of their defeat. Sir Lancelot and Sir Kay then went into the cottage and spent the rest of the night in undisturbed slumber.

Early in the morning, Lancelot slipped out of bed and quietly dressed himself in Sir Kay's armor. He took his shield as well. He then went to the stable, mounted Sir Kay's horse and rode off. When Sir Kay arose, he discovered that Sir Lancelot had taken his armor and horse and left his own in its place. At first Sir Kay was puzzled. Then he realized that, dressed in Lancelot's armor, no one would bother him. No other knight would dare attack Sir Lancelot. That meant Sir Kay would have a nice peaceful ride back to court.

Meanwhile, as Sir Lancelot was passing through a deep forest, he noticed four knights gathered in the shade of a great oak tree. They were four Knights of the Round Table: Sir Sagramour, Sir Ector, Sir Gawaine and Sir Uwaine. When they saw Lancelot approaching, they thought it was Sir Kay. Sir Sagramour decided to have some sport with Sir Kay, little realizing it was Sir Lancelot in disguise. When Sir Sagramour rode toward him, his spear at the ready, Sir Lancelot struck him so hard both man and horse fell to earth. "Did you see that?" asked Sir Ector. "He looks like a much stronger knight than Sir Kay. Watch what I do to him." But Sir Ector fared no better. Sir Lancelot felled him, too, with one powerful thrust of his spear. Next, Sir Uwaine challenged Sir Lancelot. One minute he was on his horse; the next, he was sitting in the dust, his ears ringing. For a long time Sir Uwaine did not even know where he was.

Finally, Sir Gawaine took his turn. He and Sir Lancelot gripped their spears and raced toward each other as fast as their horses could run. Crash! Sir Gawaine's spear splintered in pieces against Sir Lancelot's shield. At the same time, Sir Lancelot's spear hit Sir Gawaine such a blow that his horse fell from under him, and Gawaine barely managed to leap off to avoid being crushed.

Sir Lancelot then rode on aways, concealing a little smile, for he well knew those fellow Knights of the Round Table, but they did not know him.

The four knights were astonished. Sir Lancelot had soundly thrashed them all with one spear! That was practically unheard-of. "Whoever it is, he is a man of great might," said one of the knights. "You are certainly right about that," replied Sir Gawaine, gazing at the retreating figure of the victorious knight. "I am almost sure it is Sir Lancelot. I recognize his riding style." Still wondering, the four knights went in search of their horses, which had wandered off, and prepared for the journey back to Camelot.

Sir Lancelot, meanwhile, rode on for a long time through a dark forest. After a time, he noticed a small black dog up ahead. It seemed to be following a trail of blood through the woods. As Sir Lancelot followed along, the dog kept looking back over her shoulder, as if to make sure he was still there. Finally, they came to a great old house, surrounded by a moat. The dog ran over a bridge and into the house. Sir Lancelot followed. Inside he found himself in a great hall, and in the middle of the hall lay a dead knight. The black dog was there, licking his master's wounds.

Sir Lancelot was just wondering what to make of all this, when a woman came into the hall weeping and wringing her hands. "O knight," she moaned, "it's terrible!"

"Why, what has happened?" asked Sir Lancelot. "What befell this knight? I simply followed the dog who was following a trail of blood."

"Oh, I did not think it was you that killed my husband," said the woman sadly, "for the one who did it is severely wounded and is not likely to recover."

"What is your husband's name?" asked Lancelot.

"His name was Sir Gilbert," replied the widow, "one of the best knights of the world. I don't know the name of the man who killed him."

Seeing nothing more to do there, Sir Lancelot comforted the woman as best he could and departed. He had not gone far before he met a young woman who appeared to know him. "Thank goodness I have found you," she cried, "for I need your help badly. I know that, as a knight, you are bound to help those in need."

When Sir Lancelot asked what the trouble was, she told him that her brother had been badly wounded in a fight with Sir Gilbert. Her brother had killed Sir Gilbert in the fight, but now he was in danger of bleeding to death.

"What can I do to help?" asked Sir Lancelot.

"There is a witch who lives nearby, who told me that my brother's wounds would never heal until I found a knight who would go into the Chapel Perilous. Inside there is a sword and a dead knight wrapped in a bloody cloth. My brother will only be cured when a piece of the cloth and the sword are applied to his wounds."

"That is truly amazing," replied Sir Lancelot. "What is your brother's name?"

"His name is Sir Meliot," answered the woman.

"I am very sorry," said Sir Lancelot, "for I know him well. He is a Knight of the Round Table. I will do whatever I can to help."

"Then follow this highway. It will bring you to the Chapel Perilous," said the woman. "But please hurry! I fear for my brother's life!"

With no further ado, Sir Lancelot re-mounted his horse and rode off. In no time he was at the gate of the Chapel Perilous. He dismounted and tied his horse in the little churchyard. Then he saw something that made his blood run cold. On the front of the chapel were thirty knights' shields, each turned upside down. Many of the shields belonged to knights Sir Lancelot knew. What terrible fate had they met?

He didn't have time to wonder long, for suddenly before him were thirty huge knights, very much alive, and all dressed in black armor. They all had their swords drawn and their shields ready. Gnashing their teeth, they grinned hideously at Sir Lancelot, as if daring him to try to enter the chapel.

His heart pounding, Sir Lancelot drew his own sword and prepared to fight his way through the dreadful swarm of knights that stood in his way. But to his utter surprise, as he advanced, they stepped back, and he entered the chapel unharmed.

Inside, a single candle lit the bare stone room. Sir Lancelot could just make out a corpse covered with a silk cloth. He bent down and snipped away a piece of the cloth. As he did, it seemed to him the earth shook. Fear gripped his heart but he tried to ignore it. Then he noticed a sword on the ground near the body. He snatched it up and got out of there as fast as he could.

Outside, the same horrible knights were

waiting. They all spoke as one: "Sir Lancelot, put that sword down or you will die."

This time, Sir Lancelot was less afraid. "If you want the sword, you must fight me for it," he said. Then he walked right through them and no one raised a hand against him.

Outside the churchyard, he met a young woman. "Sir Lancelot," said she, "leave that sword behind or you must die."

"I will not leave it behind for any reason," replied Lancelot.

"You are right," said the strange young woman. "If you had left the sword behind, you would never have seen Queen Guenevere again."

"Then I would be a fool to leave it," answered the knight.

"Now," said the maiden, "I demand that you give me a kiss."

"That I cannot do," replied Lancelot.

"You are right again," she answered. "If you had kissed me your life would have ended. Then I would have kept your body with me always and cherished and preserved it. I have loved you for seven years, even though I know you love Queen Guenevere."

"God save me from your witchery," cried Sir Lancelot, "I must depart from here!" Leaping into the saddle, he rode away from the churchyard, leaving the mysterious young woman gazing after him sadly. Indeed, her unhappiness was so great that it was said she died of a broken heart shortly after.

Sir Lancelot now returned to Sir Meliot's sister, who greeted him with great joy. They went immediately to where her brother lay pale and faint from loss of blood. Sir Lancelot could see he was nearly dead.

When he saw Lancelot come into the room, Sir Meliot raised himself weakly from his bed and gasped with his last ounce of strength: "O lord, Sir Lancelot, help me!" With that, he sank back down on the pillow, his eyes closed. Sir Lancelot rushed to the bed. First, he touched the wounds with the sword from the chapel. Then he wiped the wounds with the piece of bloody cloth.

To his utter astonishment, the wounds suddenly disappeared! Sir Meliot opened his eyes and sat up. A big smile spread across his face. First he hugged his sister. Then he hugged Sir Lancelot. "It's a miracle!" he cried. "I'm well again!" Then they all three celebrated far into the night.

In the morning, Sir Lancelot departed for Camelot and the court of King Arthur. When he arrived, everyone at court turned out to greet him. When Sir Gawaine, Sir Sagramour,

Sir Ector and Sir Uwaine saw Lancelot in Sir Kay's armor, they knew it was Sir Lancelot who had beaten them all with one spear. There was much laughing and joking about it. Also present were many of the knights Sir Lancelot had freed from Sir Turquine's prison. They could not thank him enough.

Then Sir Kay told how Lancelot had rescued him from the three knights who would have killed him, and how Sir Lancelot had switched armor so that Sir Kay would not be attacked on the way home. Finally, Sir Meliot came in and told how Sir Lancelot had just recently saved him from death. After hearing about these great deeds, everyone there cheered and applauded Sir Lancelot till the rafters rang. And all agreed that he was, without doubt, the greatest knight of all.

VI
Sir Lancelot and Dame Elaine

ONE DAY, some time later, as King Arthur and the knights sat at the Round Table, a hermit came in. When the hermit saw that one of the seats at the Round Table, a seat called the Siege Perilous, was empty, he asked about it. The King and the knights told him that only one man could sit in that seat without being destroyed. "Do you know who that man is?" asked the hermit. The King and the knights admitted they did not know. "Well," said the hermit, "I know, and I tell you that he will be born this year. And there will come a time when he will sit in the Siege Perilous and he will win the Holy Grail." Having made his mysterious prediction, the hermit vanished before the King and the knights could ask him anything more.

The following day, Sir Lancelot departed from the court once again in search of adventure. Eventually, he came to a city called Corbin. In the middle of the city stood a beautiful stone tower. As he approached the tower, the people of the city began to crowd around him, for they well knew that he was Sir Lancelot, the greatest knight of the kingdom. "Sir Lancelot," they cried, "you must help us! Something terrible is happening here!"

"Why, what is wrong?" replied the noble knight.

Then the people told him about a beautiful young woman imprisoned in the tower. She had been there for five years suffering terrible torment and no one could seem to help her. Even Sir Gawaine had been there a few days before, and he could do nothing. Sir Lancelot told them that if Sir Gawaine had been unable to help, it was quite possible that he, Sir Lancelot, could not assist the lady either.

But the people would not take no for an answer and they insisted that he at least try to help the poor suffering woman. Finally, Lancelot agreed. Then they brought him to the tower, and when he came to the chamber where the lady was, the door locks unbolted as if by magic. Sir Lancelot entered and stopped in his tracks. The cell was boiling hot. Through clouds of steam he caught sight of one of the most beautiful women he had ever seen. It turned out that she had been put under a spell and imprisoned in the tower by

Morgan le Fay and the Queen of Northgalis, who were jealous of her great beauty. But astonishingly, as soon as Sir Lancelot took her by the hand, the spell was broken. Quickly he led her out of that horrible chamber.

After she had recovered a little from the shock of being rescued after all those years of torment, the lady put on new clothes. Sir Lancelot thought he had never seen anyone as pretty, unless it was Queen Guenevere.

When the people of Corbin saw that Sir Lancelot had rescued the lady in distress, they showered him with thanks. Then they told him about another problem they were having. There was a terrible dragon living in a tomb nearby. Could he slay the dragon? Sir Lancelot told them to take him there and he would do his best. When they arrived, Sir Lancelot saw these words written in gold on the tomb: "Here shall come a leopard of king's blood, and he shall slay this serpent, and this leopard shall father a lion in this country, and that lion shall excel all other knights."

Wondering what those strange words could mean, Sir Lancelot lifted the lid of the tomb. Out sprang a horrible dragon, roaring with anger and breathing fire from its mouth. Dodging the monster's searing breath, Lancelot stepped back and drew his sword. He had

Out sprang a horrible dragon, roaring with
anger and breathing fire from its mouth.

only a moment before the dragon, screeching with fury, charged forward, trying to catch Lancelot in its razor-sharp claws. But the knight was too quick for the lumbering creature, and darting in, he plunged his sword deep into the dragon's breast. With a final bloodcurdling shriek, the hideous creature fell to the ground with a great thud. Writhing in convulsions, the monster breathed its last.

While Sir Lancelot was resting from his labors, a king named Pelles approached and introduced himself. He congratulated Lancelot on killing the dragon and invited him back to his castle. Sir Lancelot accepted, for by that time he was quite tired, and hungry as well.

Soon Lancelot and King Pelles were seated at the dinner table in a great hall. A fire crackled in the great fireplace at one end of the room, which was ablaze with candles. On the table were huge platters of meat and vegetables and many other good things to eat and drink. Just as they were about to eat, a pretty young woman came in carrying a golden cup in her hands. Suddenly King Pelles and everyone else in the hall bowed their heads in prayer. "What does this mean?" asked Sir Lancelot, gazing about as a sudden hush fell over the room. Then the king told him that the cup was the holiest thing on earth. "Be well aware," the King told Sir Lancelot, "that today you have seen the Holy Grail." Everyone in the hall then turned back to their plates piled high with food and enjoyed themselves mightily.

As King Pelles sat with Sir Lancelot, he found himself wishing that the noble knight would fall in love with his daughter, Elaine. Somehow he knew that if that were to happen, Lancelot and Elaine would have a son named Galahad, a great knight who would free all captured lands and would secure the Holy Grail forever.

But the question was how to bring it about. While King Pelles wondered about this, an enchantress named Dame Brisen stole to his side and whispered in his ear. "Sir Lancelot loves only Queen Guenevere," she informed the King, "but leave it to me. I will use my magic powers to make Sir Lancelot think your daughter is Guenevere." "Do you really think you can do that?" asked the King. "Wait and see," replied the sorceress.

Later that night, Dame Brisen arranged to have a messenger come to Sir Lancelot with a ring from Queen Guenevere. "Why, where is my lady?" asked Lancelot. "At the Castle of Case," replied the messenger. "It is only five miles from here." "Well, I will go and see her there," said Lancelot, and made preparations to leave. In the meantime, Dame Brisen arranged to have the King's daughter, Elaine, go to the same castle that night.

When Sir Lancelot arrived, Dame Brisen was already there. She led him into the castle and brought him a cup of wine. No sooner had he drunk the wine than Lancelot began to feel quite strange. Little did he know that Dame Brisen had put a magic potion into the wine. Sure enough, when Elaine came into the room, Sir Lancelot imagined it was Queen Guenevere, his true love. After spending a pleasant evening together, they retired for the night.

But in the morning, when the spell had worn off, Sir Lancelot found himself with Elaine. He was very angry. He knew he had been tricked. "What kind of treachery is this?" he shouted, drawing his sword. "Who has deceived me like this?"

Frightened and ashamed, Elaine threw herself at his feet. "Oh noble knight," she cried, "take pity on me. I know I have played a trick on you but it means that I am going to have your son, who will be the noblest knight in the world." Sir Lancelot was still angry. "Why have you done this?" he cried. "Who are you?"

"I am Elaine, the daughter of King Pelles,"

replied the young woman in a trembling voice. Suddenly, Sir Lancelot realized what had happened. Feeling ashamed over his anger, he apologized. "I forgive you," he said, taking her in his arms and kissing her. "We have both been tricked by Dame Brisen. And if I ever catch her, she will lose her head by my sword."

After bidding a tender farewell to Elaine, Sir Lancelot then departed and returned to the castle at Corbin. And in due time, just as King Pelles had foreseen, his daughter Elaine gave birth to a fine young son, who was named Galahad.

Some months later, after Sir Lancelot had returned to Camelot, a rumor went around that Lancelot had a son by Elaine, the daughter of King Pelles. When Queen Guenevere heard this she was furious. She called Lancelot many names and accused him of being false to her. Then Sir Lancelot told her how he had been tricked by Dame Brisen into thinking that Elaine was Queen Guenevere. After a while, the Queen saw that he was telling the truth and she forgave him. Meanwhile, King Arthur had just returned from France where he had defeated King Claudas in a great battle. To celebrate, King Arthur announced a splendid victory feast at Camelot.

When Dame Elaine, daughter of King Pelles, heard about the feast, she asked her father's permission to go. King Pelles gave her his blessing, but insisted that she dress for the occasion in the finest clothes money could buy. When she arrived at Camelot, accompanied by a magnificent procession of twenty knights and ten ladies, King Arthur and Queen Guenevere thought she was the most beautiful and richly dressed woman who had ever come to Camelot.

But when Sir Lancelot saw her, he would not speak to her because he was still so embarrassed about threatening her with his sword that morning at the castle. Even so, he thought she was the loveliest woman he had ever seen.

When Dame Elaine realized that Lancelot was not going to speak to her, she was heart-broken, for she loved him dearly. Seeing her mistress so sad, Dame Brisen promised that she would fix everything.

That night, Queen Guenevere insisted that Dame Elaine sleep in the bedroom next to hers. Then she summoned Sir Lancelot and told him to be ready to come and see her when she called him. Sir Lancelot promised that he would. But Dame Brisen overheard their conversation and decided to play a trick on them. First, she went to Dame Elaine and told her that she would bring Sir Lancelot for a visit later that night. Dame Elaine was delighted to think that Sir Lancelot would soon be coming to see her. Then Dame Brisen, disguised as a maid, went to Sir Lancelot and told him that Queen Guenevere wanted to see him. "Please take me to her," said Lancelot. "I will gladly," replied Dame Brisen. But instead of taking him to Queen Guenevere, the crafty sorceress took him to Dame Elaine's chamber. Just before they arrived, Dame Brisen cast a magic spell over Sir Lancelot that once again made him think Dame Elaine was Queen Guenevere.

As you might guess, Queen Guenevere sent for Sir Lancelot later that evening. But, of course, Sir Lancelot was not there. At this, the Queen grew furious, for she suspected he was with Dame Elaine. "Where is that false knight?" she cried, "he has betrayed me!" No one could calm her down. Finally, when her anger had subsided, she went to bed and cried herself to sleep.

The first thing next morning, she summoned Sir Lancelot. "False knight!" she cried out as soon as she saw him, "you are a traitor. Leave my court at once and never come back!" Sir Lancelot was so taken aback by these harsh words that he felt dizzy. He had never been so unjustly accused before. He didn't know what to do. Confused and shocked, Sir Lancelot leaped out a nearby window into a garden. Then, maddened with grief, he ran toward the woods at the end of the garden and disappeared. It was the last anyone saw of him for two long years.

VII
Sir Lancelot's Exile and Return

WHEN DAME Elaine heard what had happened, she accused Queen Guenevere of chasing Sir Lancelot away. In turn, Queen Guenevere commanded Dame Elaine to leave her court immediately. In truth, both women loved Sir Lancelot very deeply and now neither one of them had him.

Queen Guenevere began to think that maybe she had acted too hastily in chasing Sir Lancelot away. She summoned three knights—Sir Bors, Sir Ector and Sir Lionel—and commanded them to search for the missing knight. Eager to find their beloved friend, the three men searched far and wide. They rode through villages and towns. They looked for him in the forest. They asked everyone they saw. But after three months, they gave up. Sir Lancelot was nowhere to be found.

Although the three knights had been unable to locate Sir Lancelot, he was indeed in the forest. Month after month he had wandered through the wild woods, living on fruit and nuts, and speaking to no one. Dressed only in shirt and trousers, he had little protection from the rain and wind. But he hardly noticed. He was out of his mind with grief and sadness over the loss of Queen Guenevere.

Then one day, purely by chance, he happened to wander into the city of Corbin. Sir Lancelot did not know it then, but Dame Elaine lived there now with their son, Galahad. But when people saw him in the street, all dirty and ragged from his time in the woods, they laughed and made fun of him. Dogs barked at this strange-looking man who had suddenly appeared in town, and small boys threw stones at him. To escape his pursuers, Lancelot climbed over a wall into the garden of a nearby castle. There he lay down beside a well and fell sound asleep.

A little while later, Dame Elaine and a few friends came into the garden to play a game. They soon noticed the sleeping man. Approaching more closely, Dame Elaine gasped. In spite of his dirty clothes and ragged appearance, she knew at once it was Sir Lancelot. Weeping with happiness, she ran to tell her father, King Pelles. The King ordered that Sir Lancelot be brought into the castle and treated with the greatest kindness.

Anyone could see that Sir Lancelot was not in his right mind and there was no telling what he might do when he awoke. They then carried him into a room in a tower that contained the cup of the Holy Grail. Sir Lancelot was laid gently down near the holy object. And because of the miraculous powers of the Grail, Sir Lancelot was cured of his madness. When he awoke, he groaned and sighed and told everyone about how sore he was.

As soon as he recognized Dame Elaine and King Pelles, Sir Lancelot begged them to tell him how he had gotten there. Then Dame Elaine explained that he had come into the city like a madman and that she and her friends had discovered him asleep by the well. Sir Lancelot marveled at this, because he remembered none of it.

After a few weeks of rest and good food, Sir Lancelot felt much better. It was time to leave the castle, but he could not go back to King Arthur's court; Queen Guenevere had forbidden that. Instead he asked Dame Elaine if her father might have a place he could use. Dame Elaine told Sir Lancelot she would ask. As luck would have it, King Pelles owned a small castle that was empty at the time. He gladly offered it to Sir Lancelot.

Soon after, Sir Lancelot, Dame Elaine and a

group of knights and ladies moved into the castle. Sir Lancelot called it Joyous Gard, or Happy Island, for the castle was surrounded on all sides by water. And although Sir Lancelot was delighted to have this beautiful place to live in, he often gazed in the direction of Camelot and a look of sadness and longing came into his eyes.

Some months later, two knights arrived outside Joyous Gard. One was Sir Percivale and the other was Sir Ector. They had both been looking for Sir Lancelot for many months, but they did not know he lived there now. Sir Percivale decided to approach the castle. Perhaps the people inside might know something of Sir Lancelot's whereabouts. Sir Ector decided to stay behind until Sir Percivale returned. So Percivale took a small boat across the moat and entered the castle. There he told a guard to tell the knight in charge that Sir Percivale wished to joust with him. When Sir Lancelot received this message, he put on his armor and prepared for battle. At a jousting place within the castle, the two knights set their spears in place and galloped towards one another. When they met, neither missed. The force of the blows knocked both knights off their horses, with a clatter. Getting to their feet, they pulled out their swords and hurtled together like two wild boars. The clanging of their great swords echoed off the great stone walls.

After fighting for almost two hours, both knights were exhausted and bleeding from their wounds. Panting for breath, Sir Percivale said, "Fair knight, I ask you to tell me your name, for I have never fought with a knight of your skill and power."

"Why, my name is Sir Lancelot," replied his opponent, "and what is yours?"

"I am Sir Percivale, son of King Pellinore and brother of Sir Lamorak and Sir Aglovale."

With that, Sir Lancelot groaned and threw his sword and shield away from him. "Good grief," he exclaimed, "why am I fighting with a fellow Knight of the Round Table?"

Then Sir Percivale realized that it truly was Sir Lancelot. He begged Lancelot to forgive him and told him that Sir Ector was waiting outside the castle. They immediately sent for Sir Ector. When he came in, Sir Ector and Lancelot hugged like long-lost brothers. Then all three went into the castle and spent the evening catching up on everything that had happened. Sir Percivale and Sir Ector asked Sir Lancelot if he was ever going to return to King Arthur's court.

"No," replied Sir Lancelot sadly. "I have been forbidden by the Queen."

Then Sir Ector and Sir Percivale told Lancelot how much King Arthur and Queen Guenevere missed him, not to mention all the other knights and ladies of the court. After much persuasion, Sir Lancelot finally gave in. "I will go with you," he said.

When Dame Elaine heard about his departure, she was very unhappy. But she loved him too much to stand in his way and so she let him go.

Five days later, the three knights arrived at Camelot. When the arrival of Sir Lancelot was announced, the court went mad with joy. A great feast was prepared and King Arthur and Queen Guenevere and all the knights and ladies attended. At the feast, Sir Percivale and Sir Ector told about all that had happened to Sir Lancelot. And as they related his adventures, Queen Guenevere cried for happiness. Then King Arthur spoke: "I am curious about why you went mad, Sir Lancelot. I and many others thought it was because of your love for Dame Elaine. We hear that you and she have a son named Galahad who shows great promise."

"My lord," replied Lancelot, "if I have acted foolishly, I have paid dearly for it." The King wondered what he meant by that, but he said no more about it. Everyone else at court, though, knew why Sir Lancelot had gone mad, and over whom. But now it was time to celebrate and all the lords and ladies gladly passed the rest of the night in feasting and merrymaking.

Not long after, Queen Guenevere decided to give a special dinner for the Knights of the Round Table. She invited twenty-four of her favorite knights to the dinner, and to make it even more special, she decided to prepare the meal herself. Now, one of the knights invited was Sir Gawaine. He was a great favorite of the Queen, who knew that above all other foods, Sir Gawaine enjoyed fresh fruit. With that in mind, Queen Guenevere made certain there was plenty of fruit on the table when the knights sat down to eat.

Unfortunately, Sir Gawaine had an enemy at court. His name was Sir Pinel, and he hated Sir Gawaine because Gawaine had killed his brother in a tournament. Now Sir Pinel saw his chance for revenge. Knowing that Sir Gawaine loved fruit, Sir Pinel crept quietly into the dining hall before dinner and poisoned the fruit near Sir Gawaine's place at the table.

Soon after, all the knights came in and took their places. Queen Guenevere welcomed them all and thanked them for coming. She was a little sad, however, for Sir Lancelot was not there. She and Sir Lancelot had quarreled and the great knight had decided to leave Camelot for a while.

Meanwhile, the knights were eating hungrily, complimenting Queen Guenevere on the meal she had prepared with her own hands. Then something terrible happened. Sir Patrice, a cousin of Sir Mador, took an apple and ate it. Almost immediately, he gasped, his hands clutching at his throat. The other knights rushed to his side, but it was too late. With a groan of agony, Sir Patrice closed his eyes and died.

Suddenly everyone turned and stared at Queen Guenevere. They knew Sir Patrice had been poisoned and she had cooked the meal! Sir Gawaine spoke first: "My Queen, everyone knows how much I like fruit. Therefore, it seems to me that this poison was meant for me!" Queen Guenevere was so shocked at this, she could not utter a word. Then Sir Mador spoke up: "My cousin has been murdered and I demand revenge. I think the Queen is guilty!"

At this, the Queen burst into tears and sank into a chair, hiding her face in her hands. All the noise and commotion brought King Arthur to the dining hall in a hurry. "What's going on?" he demanded. When the knights explained

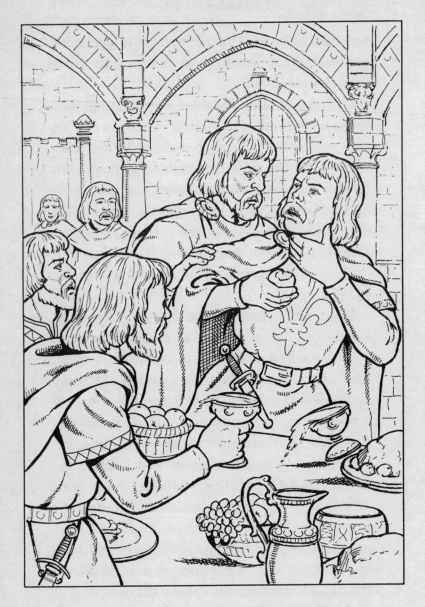

Almost immediately, he gasped, his hands
clutching at his throat.

what had happened, King Arthur was upset and angry. Since Queen Guenevere had prepared the food herself, it looked very bad. And all the while, Sir Mador continued to accuse her.

"My lords," said King Arthur, "I do not believe the Queen did this terrible thing, but I cannot very well defend her myself, because she is my wife. I am sure," continued the King, looking around at the stern and angry knights before him, "that a worthy knight will defend my Queen and save her from a death sentence!"

"King Arthur," replied Sir Mador, "none of the knights here will defend her because they all think she is guilty."

The knights agreed that this was so. By this time, Queen Guenevere had recovered a little. "I swear on my honor to everyone here that I did nothing wrong!" cried the tearful Queen. "It is true I prepared the meal, but I did not poison anyone!"

"My lord," said Sir Mador, "I demand that you decide on a day of justice. That day, the Queen's champion must meet me in battle. If I win, the Queen is guilty and must be burned at the stake. If I lose, the Queen may go free."

Reluctantly, King Arthur agreed to the terms, for that is how questions of guilt or innocence were decided in those days. With a heavy heart, King Arthur set a day two weeks from then as the Queen's day of judgment. On that day, in a meadow beside Westminster, the Queen's champion would meet Sir Mador in battle. If he lost, the Queen would die.

Later, when they were alone, King Arthur asked his wife how the whole thing had come about. "I tell you I don't know anything about it," she said.

"Where is Sir Lancelot?" asked King Arthur. "He would defend you."

"I don't know where he is," responded the Queen sadly. "They tell me he is nowhere to be found in Camelot."

"Then send for Sir Bors," said the King. "Perhaps he will agree to help."

As King Arthur suggested, Queen Guenevere met with Sir Bors and threw herself on his mercy. But Sir Bors was reluctant to assist the Queen because he knew what the other knights would think. But finally, after much persuasion, he agreed to be the Queen's champion. But only if no other knight came to her rescue. The Queen was overjoyed. "Oh thank you, Sir Bors!" she cried, "you will not regret this!"

After leaving the Queen, Sir Bors rode straight to a hermit's hut in the woods. He happened to know Sir Lancelot was staying there. He told Sir Lancelot all that had happened. "Go to the battlefield on the appointed day," said Lancelot, "but delay the fight a little until you see me come. I have a plan." Sir Bors agreed and left Lancelot in the hermit's hut.

On the appointed day, King Arthur and Queen Guenevere and all the Knights of the Round Table gathered in the meadow at Westminster to watch the contest. Nearby was a great iron stake surrounded by firewood. If Sir Mador won, the Queen would be burned at the stake. If Sir Bors won, she would be free.

It was time, at last. The two knights rode to opposite ends of the field and prepared for battle. As Sir Bors placed his spear in position, he noticed a knight riding toward him from a little wood near the edge of the field. He was astride a splendid white horse and carried a shield with strange markings. When he reached Sir Bors, the knight spoke: "Fair knight, allow me to do battle in your place. I have ridden hard to be here this day and I beg you to do as we agreed a short time ago."

"Gladly," replied Sir Bors, delighted to be relieved of a fight he did not want. He then rode to where King Arthur was sitting and explained that the knight on the white horse had offered to fight in his place.

"Who is he?" asked King Arthur.

"I don't know," replied Sir Bors, "but he has kindly offered to be the Queen's champion."

"Very well," said the King, beginning to grow impatient at the delay. "Let the contest begin!"

When both knights were in position, a trumpet blast sounded and the two charged toward each other as hard as they could. With a mighty crash, Sir Mador's spear splintered in a hundred pieces, but the other knight's spear held and he knocked Sir Mador backwards over the tail of his horse. With a great clatter, Sir Mador landed on his back in the dirt. But quick as lightning, he leaped to his feet and drew his sword. "Get off your horse and fight me on foot!" he cried.

"Very well," responded the other knight, nimbly jumping down and pulling out his own sword. The two then fought like madmen, each giving the other many terrible blows. But at last, the other knight dealt Sir Mador a mighty blow on the side of the helmet that knocked him head over heels. While he lay there, dizzy from the ringing in his ears, the other knight reached down and yanked off his helmet.

"I surrender," gasped Sir Mador, "you are too strong. I beg you to spare my life."

"On one condition," replied the other knight softly: "that you drop all charges against

Queen Guenevere and never mention the matter again."

"It shall be as you wish," whispered Sir Mador. Then, in a louder voice that everyone could hear, he agreed to take back all that he had said against the Queen.

With that, the fight was over. The Queen was saved. "Hurrah!" shouted the crowd as the victorious knight made his way to the stand where King Arthur and Queen Guenevere were waiting to greet him. After the King and Queen had both thanked the knight profusely, the King invited him to take off his helmet and have some refreshment. "Well!" exclaimed the King, "it's none other than Sir Lancelot!" Once again, the greatest Knight of the Round Table had won a noble victory. When she saw who it was that had saved her life, Queen Guenevere shed many tears of joy and gratitude. All the other Knights of the Round Table gathered round and clapped Lancelot on the back. King Arthur shook his hand again and again.

Later on, it was discovered that Sir Pinel was actually the one who had poisoned the apples. When he found out his crime had been brought to light, he fled the kingdom in disgrace. Even Sir Mador was forgiven, after Sir Lancelot had put in a good word for him, and once again, peace reigned in Camelot.

VIII

The Death of King Arthur

BUT UNFORTUNATELY, those golden days of harmony in the court of King Arthur came to an end all too soon. It happened in this way: because Sir Lancelot and Queen Guenevere were such good friends, they spent a lot of time together, talking and enjoying each other's company. After a time, people who were enemies of Sir Lancelot planted the seed of jealousy in King Arthur's heart. And as time went on, he grew angrier and more jealous with each passing day, until finally he threatened to have Queen Guenevere put to death if she continued to see Sir Lancelot.

The Queen was very frightened. After talking with Sir Lancelot, they decided to leave Camelot and go to Joyous Gard, Sir Lancelot's castle. At least the Queen would be safe there until King Arthur calmed down. But instead, the Queen's departure had just the opposite effect: King Arthur was enraged. Gathering his knights about him, he vowed to lay siege to Joyous Gard until Sir Lancelot should restore the Queen to him.

In a short time King Arthur had gathered a strong army and marched right up to the walls of Sir Lancelot's great stone castle. Meanwhile, Lancelot had heard about the King's plans to attack, and had gathered his own army of knights who were loyal to him. When word came that King Arthur's army was approaching the gates, Sir Lancelot went to a high tower and looked down. King Arthur saw him immediately and shouted: "Come out, if you dare, and meet me in battle!"

"My lord," replied Sir Lancelot, "I will never fight with the noble King who made me a knight!"

"Never mind your pretty words," sneered the King, "you have dishonored my Queen and taken her by force."

Then Sir Lancelot reminded King Arthur of how he had saved the Queen from death when she was falsely accused by Sir Mador and how he and the King had been good and loyal friends for many years. At first, King Arthur seemed to listen, but then Sir Gawaine and other enemies of Sir Lancelot persuaded him that Lancelot was an evil knight who must be punished. And so it was decided that King

Arthur and his men would meet Sir Lancelot and his knights in battle the very next day.

As soon as it was light, the two armies came together with a great crashing of spears and shields. All day the battle raged, with many knights slain on both sides. And always King Arthur looked for a chance to slay Sir Lancelot. But as soon as he managed to get near Sir Lancelot, that knight moved away—not because he was afraid, but because he did not want to fight against the King he still loved and respected.

Finally, Sir Bors, who was on Lancelot's side, challenged King Arthur to fight. "With pleasure!" cried the King, spurring his horse forward. But to his great surprise, Sir Bors knocked him off his horse with one blow. As King Arthur lay stunned in the dust, Sir Bors drew his sword and looked at Sir Lancelot as if to say, "Shall I end this war right here and now?"

"No," cried Sir Lancelot, "I will not stand by and let you kill the noble King who made me a knight!"

With that, he jumped off his horse, pulled King Arthur to his feet and helped him back on his own horse. With great feeling, Sir Lancelot spoke: "For God's sake, my King, let us stop fighting. This war will do nobody any good!"

King Arthur looked sadly down at the knight he had loved so well. He thought to himself about Sir Lancelot's courage and kindness, even in the heat of battle, and the words stuck in his throat. Unable to speak and unable to bear the sight of Lancelot any longer, he turned away with tears in his eyes and rode from the battlefield. The fighting was over for that day.

During the siege of Joyous Gard, news of the fighting reached the Pope in Rome. Disturbed by the reports of battle and bloodshed between such old friends as King Arthur and Sir Lancelot, the Pope decided to use his influence to help stop the war. He sent urgent messages to them both, urging them to forget their differences and to make peace. And he asked Sir Lancelot to return Queen Guenevere to the King.

It worked. Both sides agreed to stop fighting and Sir Lancelot promised to bring Queen Guenevere back to Camelot. And so it happened. On a beautiful spring day, Sir Lancelot and Queen Guenevere set out on their journey, each splendidly dressed in white cloth with gold embroidery. Along with them rode a hundred knights, all dressed in green, each holding an olive branch as a sign of peace.

When they arrived, Sir Lancelot led Queen

Guenevere before the King. With great ceremony, Lancelot explained that there had been
many lies told about him and the Queen. And
once again he reminded the King of all the
services he had performed in the past. When
he was through speaking, everyone there realized the truth of what he had said, and many
wept for happiness to see the King and Queen
together again.

But there was one knight who was not
happy. Sir Gawaine could not forgive Sir
Lancelot because Lancelot had slain his
brother, Sir Gaheris, during the fighting. Even
though Sir Lancelot had not realized it
was Sir Gaheris, Sir Gawaine nevertheless
privately vowed to revenge himself on Sir
Lancelot as soon as he got the chance.

Sir Lancelot looked about sadly and then he
spoke: "I am greatly saddened by all that has
happened, and I think it might be best if I left
this noble fellowship of knights forever." Then
he turned to Queen Guenevere: "I bid you
farewell, my Queen. Speak well of me, and if
you ever need my help, you have only to ask."
Then, with a last wave to the knights and
ladies of the court, Sir Lancelot slowly rode
out through the gates of Camelot. It was the
beginning of the end of the fellowship of the
Knights of the Round Table.

After leaving the court, Sir Lancelot returned to Joyous Gard and from there, he traveled over the sea to the land of Benwick, where he also had a castle. There he lived with many of the knights who had been loyal to him during his battles with King Arthur. Unfortunately, those battles were not over yet. After Sir Lancelot had left Camelot, Sir Gawaine again managed to persuade the king that Sir Lancelot was a traitor. King Arthur decided to take an army and pursue Sir Lancelot in Benwick. Before he left, King Arthur put Morgan le Fay's son, Sir Mordred, in charge of the kingdom.

But Sir Mordred was an evil man. Secretly, he wanted to get rid of King Arthur, crown himself King and marry Queen Guenevere. So he told all the knights at Camelot a terrible lie. He told them that King Arthur had been killed in a battle with Sir Lancelot. Then Sir Mordred persuaded the knights to appoint him King. When King Arthur heard what Mordred had done, he was furious. He immediately made plans to return to England.

When King Arthur and his army landed at Dover, Sir Mordred was there with an army of his own. In the great battle that followed, King Arthur's forces defeated Sir Mordred, but Sir Gawaine was fatally wounded. As he lay near death, he told King Arthur that none of this would have happened if he hadn't insisted that the King pursue Sir Lancelot into Benwick. After urging the King to send for Sir Lancelot and make peace with him, Sir Gawaine died. King Arthur was broken-hearted. The two knights he had loved the most, Sir Gawaine and Sir Lancelot, were both gone from him, and that in the bitterest of circumstances.

He had little time to worry about it, however, for Sir Mordred and his army had issued a new challenge to King Arthur. This time King Arthur and Sir Mordred were to bring their armies to Salisbury and there they would face each other again. The night before the battle, King Arthur dreamed that the ghost of Sir Gawaine warned him that if he fought the next day, he would be killed. But he put the warning out of his mind as a bad dream and soon forgot about it.

The next day, both armies came together in furious battle. The air was filled with the sounds of sword on sword and spears crashing against shields. Many knights on both sides had already been killed when King Arthur spotted Sir Mordred leaning on his sword near some fallen knights. Snatching up a great spear, he ran toward Sir Mordred, crying "Traitor! This day you will die!"

When he saw King Arthur coming, Sir Mordred quickly raised his sword and ran to meet him. With a mighty thrust, King Arthur plunged his spear into Sir Mordred, just below his shield. At the same time, Sir Mordred struck Arthur a terrible blow on the head with his sword. The blade split his helmet wide open and pierced King Arthur's brain.

Sir Mordred fell to the ground, dead. King Arthur, badly wounded, was helped by a young knight off the field where he could rest. "Ah, Sir Lancelot," groaned the King in great pain, "I needed you today. I am sorry I was ever against you, for I fear I am going to die as Sir Gawaine warned me in my dream."

Then King Arthur called one of his knights, Sir Bedivere, to his side. "Sir Bedivere," said the King, "take my sword, Excalibur, and throw it in that lake you see yonder. Then come back and tell me what you saw there." Sir Bedivere did as he was told. When he reached the lake, he threw the sword as far as he could out over the water. To his astonishment, an arm, clad all in white, rose out of the water and caught the sword in mid-air. Then, as Sir Bedivere watched, the arm shook the sword three times and disappeared beneath the waves.

Shaking with disbelief, Sir Bedivere hurried back to King Arthur and told him what he had seen. "Take me there immediately," gasped the King, "for I fear I have waited too long." Sir Bedivere obeyed the King's orders and led the dying monarch to the waterside. There, floating gently near the shore, was a beautiful barge, draped in colorful silks and decorated with precious jewels. And in the barge were three queens: Queen Morgan le Fay, Arthur's sister, the Queen of Northgalis and the Queen of the Waste Lands. Also in the barge was the Lady of the Lake, who had done so much for Arthur. Slowly and gently, Sir Bedivere helped King Arthur into the barge. Morgan le Fay cradled the King's head in her lap and spoke gently to him. Then the boat began to move away from the shore. Sir Bedivere shouted after the King, "My lord Arthur, what shall I do now that you're leaving me here with my enemies?"

Weakly, the King raised his head and replied: "Do the best you can, for I cannot help you any more. I am going to the Vale of Avalon to be healed of my wound."

And with that, the barge slowly vanished into the mists hovering over the lake, taking with it the noble Arthur, founder and leader of the Knights of the Round Table and the greatest of all Kings.

That night, four ladies were spied bringing a corpse into a tomb in the chapel at Canterbury, lighting a hundred candles around it,

There, floating gently near the shore, was a
beautiful barge.

and leaving behind a thousand gold-pieces for the bishop. Everyone knew whose body it was, and above the tomb was written:

HERE LIES ARTHUR, THE ONCE AND FUTURE KING.

Later, when Queen Guenevere heard that King Arthur, Sir Mordred and many other knights had been killed, she fell into a deep sadness. Because of this sadness and perhaps because she felt that she herself had caused a great deal of unhappiness, the Queen decided to devote herself to a religious life. Leaving the court and giving up her crown, she went to a convent in Almesbury where she spent her days praying and doing good deeds.

When Sir Lancelot heard the news of King Arthur's death, he, too, was greatly saddened. He returned to England, where he learned of all that had happened. After paying his respects at Sir Gawaine's tomb, Sir Lancelot went to Almesbury to see Queen Guenevere. Although she was glad to see him, Guenevere found that just looking at him reminded her of all the terrible things that had happened and of the death of King Arthur. And though it was very painful for her, she asked him to leave and not to return. Sir Lancelot felt as if his heart would break, but he understood why they had to part. Before he left, he promised Guenevere that he, too, would devote himself to a life of prayer and service. Then, sadly, he departed from Queen Guenevere for the last time.

Not long after Sir Lancelot had left, Queen Guenevere fell ill. She was unable to get her strength back, and within a short time, the unhappy woman passed out of this life. Just before she died, she asked that Sir Lancelot be summoned and that after her death he bury her beside King Arthur. When he learned that Guenevere was dying, Sir Lancelot rushed to her side, but he arrived a half hour too late. With a heavy heart, Lancelot did as she requested and saw to it that her body was laid in King Arthur's tomb.

Then, weary and dejected, the grieving knight returned to Joyous Gard. Now that both Guenevere and King Arthur were dead, Sir Lancelot found himself with little reason to live. Nearly everyone he loved and cared about was gone. As time went by, he began eating less and less. Over the months, his body slowly wasted away. Finally, he, too, became very sick and in his weakened condition he could not get well. Soon after, Sir Lancelot died. His body was prepared for burial at Joyous Gard as he had wished. And as his loyal knights stood weeping over his tomb, Sir Ector murmured these final words:

"You were never defeated in battle by any earthly knight. You were the truest friend we ever had. You were always courteous and gentle with women, and you were stern, but fair, with your enemies. You were the greatest knight of all and we shall not look upon your like again."

THE END